2/7/92

To Michael —
   Best wishes to a new young friend!
I hope that this old-fashioned St. Nick.
will bring you an "ark-full" of happiness —
enough to last you a lifetime!
   HAPPY SAILING ON THE CHRISTMAS ARK
      ANY DAY OF THE YEAR!
   Your friend,
                    Robert D. San Souci

THE CHRISTMAS ARK

ROBERT D. SAN SOUCI

ILLUSTRATED BY
DANIEL SAN SOUCI

DOUBLEDAY

NEW YORK   LONDON   TORONTO   SYDNEY   AUCKLAND

AUTHOR'S NOTE:

The name of the ship, *Queen Calafia,* is the name of the ruler of a mythical island, called "California," first mentioned in a popular Spanish novel written in 1510 by Montalvo. In that adventure story, the island is found to be ruled by black warrior women—"amazons"—who wear gold ornaments, carry gold weapons, and tame wild beasts for transportation.

"Know that on the right hand of the Indies, there is an island called California," wrote Montalvo, adding that it was "very near to the terrestrial paradise."

From this tale came the name of the Golden State—and the name of the ship on which Sarah and Elizabeth journeyed to California.

PUBLISHED BY DOUBLEDAY a division of Bantam Doubleday Dell Publishing Group, Inc. 666 Fifth Avenue, New York, New York 10103 DOUBLEDAY and the portrayal of an anchor with a dolphin are trademarks of Doubleday, a division of Bantam Doubleday Dell Publishing Group, Inc. Library of Congress Cataloging-in-Publication Data San Souci, Robert D. The Christmas ark. Summary: A Christmas Eve journey with a nautical Santa on his gift-laden ark uplifts the heart of a lonely girl. [1. Santa Claus—Fiction. 2. Christmas—Fiction] I. San Souci, Daniel, ill. II. Title. PZ7.S1947Ch 1991 [Fic] 88-30908

ISBN 0-385-24836-9 ISBN 0-385-24837-7 (lib. bdg.)

Text copyright © 1991 by Robert D. San Souci Illustrations copyright © 1991 by Daniel San Souci

RL: 3.2

MERRY CHRISTMAS
to my niece and godchild,
Andrea Cebalo
—R.S.S.

TO THE FACULTY AND STUDENTS
of St. Theresa's School,
Oakland, California
—D.S.S.

"This is an *awful* Christmas Eve," declared nine-year-old Elizabeth Branscombe. She was leaning over the rail of the *Queen Calafia* and frowning at the fog swirling around the ship.

"Oh, Tessie, I *wish* you wouldn't be such a killjoy," said her younger sister Sarah. "It makes things so much worse."

"Well, they *are* worse!" cried Elizabeth. "We shouldn't be stuck on the ocean the night before Christmas with nothing but fog, fog, fog."

"It's not so bad," said Sarah, trying to sound cheerful. But it wasn't easy, since she felt almost as unhappy. Nothing had seemed right since their father sold the farm in Maine. He had gone to build a new life for them in California, where gold had been discovered two years earlier.

As it turned out, Jonathan Branscombe's latest letter to his anxious family in Maine told them that he was now partner in a dry goods store in San Francisco. This, he promised, would provide them with a better life than chasing after gold.

So the girls and their mother had been traveling by ship for months. Their plan was to arrive in San Francisco before Christmas, but bad weather had delayed them. Now, only a day from being reunited with their father, they were fogbound and drifting at sea.

"I *hate* this fog!" said Elizabeth, pushing a few moist curls under her bonnet, which was limp from the damp. Sarah, who was nearly a mirror image of her sister, pushed a stray brown curl of her own out of sight.

"We can't have Christmas in the middle of the ocean," added Elizabeth. "St. Nicholas will never find us!"

Worried, Sarah asked, "Do you really think St. Nicholas won't come?"

"Of course he'll come," said their mother, who had been talking with another passenger. She gave both girls a hug, but warned Elizabeth, "Older sisters who tease younger sisters might just find a lump of coal in their stockings. Now both of you come along, and we'll go below for dinner."

"Yes, ma'am," said Elizabeth, taking her mother's hand.

But Sarah, taking her mother's other hand, found herself wondering how St. Nicholas could possibly find his way through the thick, cottony fog.

That night, in their tiny cabin, Mother sewed while Elizabeth, one leg dangling from her upper bunk, read a book. Sarah, on her own narrow bunk, played with her favorite toy: a little wooden ark filled with carved wooden animals—two of each—and a tiny Noah and his wife. It had been a gift from St. Nicholas the year before. Noah, with his white beard and painted smile, reminded Sarah of the jolly elf.

"Are you sure St. Nicholas can find us at sea?" asked Sarah.

Her mother smiled. "Of course. I've heard he's the special friend of sailors as well as children. I'm sure he could sail through this fog as well as the best sea captain."

"And, maybe he has a ship like my ark," said Sarah, holding her toy up in the air. "Only, instead of animals, it would be filled with presents for children all around the world."

"That's silly," said Elizabeth, never looking up from her book. "St. Nicholas has a sleigh. *Everyone* knows that."

"Well, whether he comes by ship or sleigh, it's time for bed," said Mother, setting aside her sewing. "Or St. Nicholas won't come at all."

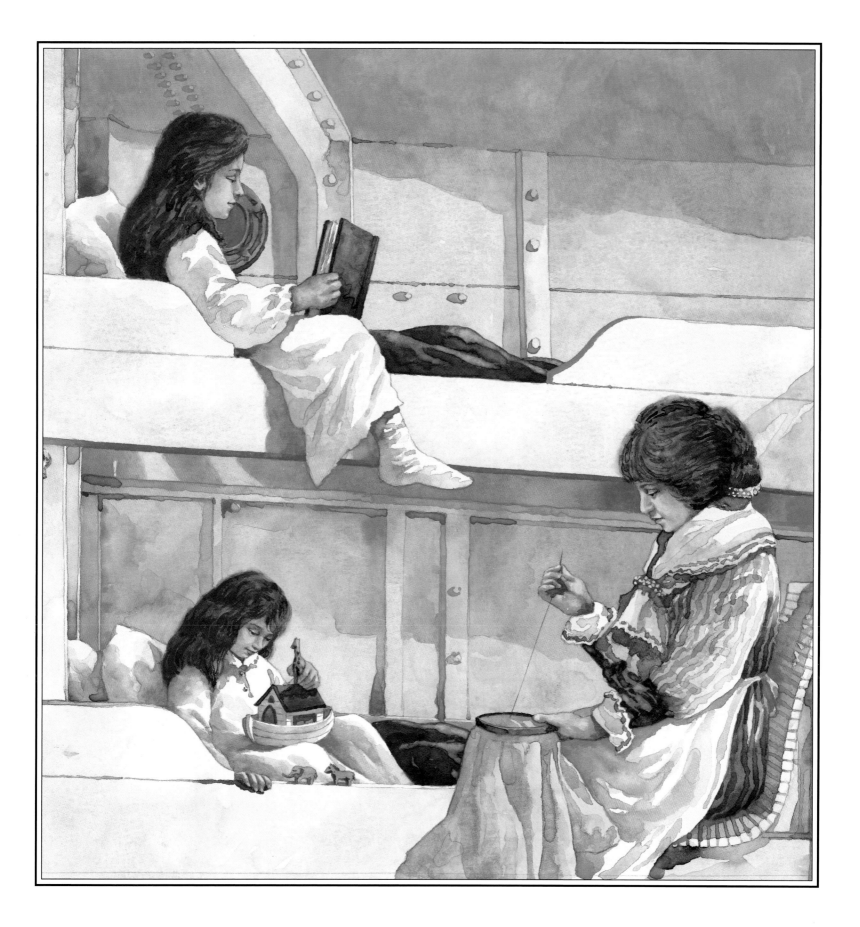

During the night, Sarah woke suddenly from a dream of Christmas in Maine. She was surprised to see a brilliant silver light pouring through the round porthole high overhead.

Her mother and sister slept on, undisturbed by the light. Sarah quietly put on her cape and bonnet. Then she went up on deck. There she discovered that no one was keeping watch over the dreaming *Queen Calafia*.

But the most amazing thing was the light that blazed down through the fog. Excited and afraid at once, Sarah watched a bubble of silver—bigger and brighter than the moon—descend toward the ship.

"*What* is *that?*" someone asked. Turning, Sarah saw Elizabeth, rubbing her eyes, her bonnet tied crookedly.

"Did the light wake you, too?" asked Sarah.

"No, *you* did," Elizabeth said as the two girls stared into the light. Then she whispered, "Is the moon falling?"

Before Sarah could answer, a huge ark, blazing with silver light, appeared from out of the foggy sky. Silently and gently as a snowflake, it settled on the sea and drifted toward the *Queen Calafia*. The sisters, squeezing each other's hand in wonder, saw that the ship's rails were lined with elfin sailors.

The ark drew alongside the *Queen Calafia*. Elfin hands extended a shining gangplank with lifelines of silver cording along both sides. Then the captain of the ark appeared at the other end.

He wore a weatherbeaten red peacoat buttoned all the way up under his snow-white beard, and a well-worn red cap perched on his curly white hair. A gold telescope was stuffed in one pocket and a silver-bound notebook in the other.

He had the merriest smile and the reddest cheeks Sarah had ever seen. Touching his white-gloved fingers to the brim of his cap in a salute, he said, "Sarah Branscombe, I presume?"

"Yes, I am!" said Sarah. "And this is Tessie—I mean, Elizabeth. But who are you?"

"Well, many people call me St. Nicholas. And I've come here tonight to invite you aboard my Christmas ark to travel with me around the world. Every Christmas, I choose one child to make the journey with me. But—oh, dear!—now there are *two* of you. This is most unusual."

"*I* woke Tessie up," said Sarah.

"She did," said Elizabeth. "But I'd like to come too if I may."

"Oh, my," sighed St. Nicholas. "This is all *very* irregular. You see, the child I choose to travel with me gets to pick one Christmas out of all those they see to be his or her own special Christmas."

"Please let Tessie come," Sarah begged. "Or *no* Christmas would seem quite right, because I'd know how sad she'd feel to be left behind."

"Very well," said St. Nicholas. "But I can only give *one* special Christmas, so it will have to be the one you *both* want."

"Oh, thank you!" the sisters cried.

"You're quite welcome, I'm sure. Now then, come along, and we'll be on our way."

When they stood safely on the deck of the ark, St. Nicholas took the huge wheel at the front and guided the ship away from the *Queen Calafia.*

"How does the ark move without sails?" wondered Sarah.

"How does it stay in one place without an anchor?" asked Elizabeth.

"You'll find my ark goes where I want it to go quickly enough, and stays where I want it to stay," said St. Nick. "Now, hold on to the rail; we're on our way west."

He pulled back on the wheel, and the ark rose rapidly into the sky. Soon the *Queen Calafia* was lost far below and behind in a cloud of fog, while the ark raced against the moon high above.

The ark's first stop was the Sandwich Islands, where the Hawaiian people lived. There St. Nick brought the vessel to rest on a moonlit bay. In the distance, Sarah and Elizabeth saw a town nestled amid palm trees and banana plants.

The sisters helped St. Nick's elves load a small gold boat with presents. Then they flew through the air, from rooftop to rooftop, while St. Nicholas left presents for the island children.

Later, they sailed high above a volcano. In its glow, the sisters saw each other's face turn as red as St. Nick's own.

Then they continued on to Australia, where they visited cities along the coast, then flew inland toward the sheep ranches, miles from the sea.

Below, kangaroos, their fur turned silver by the ark's bright sheen, leaped across the grasslands, drawn to the flying ship.

"It feels like summer," said Sarah.

"That's because it *is* summer in this part of the world," St. Nick said.

"What fun it would be to have a Christmas picnic!" cried Sarah. "We could go bathing at the shore. That would be a *perfect* holiday—Christmas and summer rolled into one! I'll say yes, if you will," she told Elizabeth.

But Elizabeth said, "No—that wouldn't feel like Christmas *at all* to me."

So on they flew, to tiny islands, to Japan, and to the cities of China, where the ark sailed above a sea of tile roofs with upcurved corners, like frozen waves.

This time, Elizabeth said, "Can't we stay and have our Christmas here? We can wear silk robes and satin slippers and fly kites. You could have a silk dragon kite, and I could have one shaped like a butterfly."

But Sarah shook her head, saying, "No, I don't think this is the right place yet."

Africa came next. They drifted across sandy deserts, where camels, tied beside huge tents, gazed up at them. Then they glided over jungles far to the south. A lion roared to mark their passing, and when the ark landed on a broad, dark river, a hippopotamus bellowed and some crocodiles snapped their jaws. At the sound, Sarah laughed, while Elizabeth gasped and clutched at her sister's hand.

"They're only saying 'Merry Christmas' in their own way," chuckled St. Nicholas.

But Elizabeth would not let go of Sarah's hand, even so.

In the golden rowboat, the sisters and St. Nick visited trading posts along the river, leaving gifts for the families there.

"It would be exciting to spend Christmas here," said Sarah. "Think of having Christmas with wonderful animals all around. Say yes, Tessie, and we can have a real holiday adventure."

But Elizabeth shook her head. "I don't fancy becoming a lion's Christmas dinner, thank you."

Sarah sighed and wondered if her sister would *ever* agree with her.

They soared above the great cities of Europe, above farming towns and fishing villages, fields and forests, canals and rivers. They crossed the English Channel, where the wind set their capes fluttering and forced them to tie extra knots in their bonnet ribbons, so they wouldn't lose them.

In England, they helped St. Nicholas bring toys to a grand manor. As the household slept, they gazed in wonder at the beautiful tree decorated with sugarplums and sweets in the shape of apples, pears, and walnuts. Outside, snow was falling, while a glowing fire, behind an elegant screen, kept the room snug and cozy.

"This is perfect," said Elizabeth. "It's just like the Christmases I've read about in books. Say yes, and we'll spend Christmas here," she begged her sister.

Sarah thought for a while before she decided. "No, something is still missing for me."

"Oh, Sarah!" cried Elizabeth in disappointment.

Across the sea to South America they flew. They visited villages along the Amazon River, on the Argentine plains, and high in the Andes. For a moment, Sarah was tempted to spend Christmas in the lovely mountains. But even before she asked, Elizabeth, still unhappy about not spending Christmas in England, said, "No."

St. Nicholas, constantly calling orders to his elfin crew or checking his silver-bound notebook or peering through his golden telescope, did not seem to notice that the sisters had moved to opposite sides of the ark and would not look at each other.

But when the ship reached America, and they saw the rocky coast of Maine below them, the girls quickly forgot their anger. They hugged each other, excited by the familiar sight.

"That's our farm!" cried Sarah, pointing to the small house and barn outside powdery fields bounded by ice-crusted fences.

"How pretty the snow looks," said Elizabeth. "It still feels like home."

Eagerly, they climbed into the golden rowboat. They flew in a trice from the ark to the snow-covered roof of the house they had once lived in. Then they were down the chimney.

While St. Nick filled the stockings, the girls gazed delightedly at the decorated Christmas tree and savored the faint lingering smells of the roast turkey and mince pie that had been served at dinner. Then they wiped matching circles in the frosty windowpane to gaze out at the familiar snowscape.

"Let's choose *this* for our Christmas," said Elizabeth. "Surely this is the best Christmas of all."

"No," said Sarah sadly. "It feels *nice* to be here. But this house belongs to someone else now. And it just wouldn't feel right to have Christmas here without Mamma and Papa."

"Oh!" wailed Elizabeth. "You're impossible!"

"Come now, take my hand," said St. Nicholas. "It's time we were getting back to the ark."

"Please, can I have Christmas here, even if Sarah doesn't want to?" Elizabeth asked St. Nick.

But he just shook his head. "You must both want it, or the wish won't come true."

Reluctantly, Elizabeth joined hands with the others. In an instant, they were back on the roof, beside the golden boat. They returned to the ark in silence.

From Maine, they traveled westward across America, stopping at cities and towns, at grand plantations and sod houses and even a Mississippi riverboat. They stopped at a circled wagon train, swept high above the Rocky Mountains, and visited mining towns in California's gold country.

One of their last stops was San Francisco.

"I have something special to show you," said St. Nick with a wink.

Very soon, the girls found themselves in a small hotel room. A man was asleep in a big chair, with a blanket drawn around him.

"Papa!" the girls cried, but their father slept on.

"He can't hear you," St. Nick explained. "We're a dream to him."

A small Christmas tree had been set on a table near the room's single window. Stacked around it were gaily wrapped packages—many of them with tags reading "Sarah" and "Elizabeth." Curled up in a basket under the table were two kittens. The basket had both their names painted on it.

"He's gotten us kittens!" said Sarah. "I've always wanted one."

"Oh, so have I," said Elizabeth, kneeling down next to her sister to get a closer look at the tiny creatures.

The kittens opened their eyes and purred softly.

"Animals can see things that people can't," St. Nick said with a smile.

"Papa has Christmas waiting for us," said Sarah, "just as soon as we get here." After a minute, she added, "I know now what Christmas I want! I want to be back on the boat with Mamma, because that's going to become this Christmas, too—when we land."

"And you, Elizabeth?" asked St. Nick. "Is this the Christmas you want?"

"Oh, yes!" she answered softly, slowly stroking each of the kittens.

Dawn was just beginning to break when they returned to the *Queen Calafia*. The girls were happy to see that the winds had scattered the fog. The ship would be able to reach San Francisco very soon.

Sarah and Elizabeth gave St. Nick a hug each, then ran across the silver gangplank to the deck of the *Queen Calafia*. They waved to the ark as it flew north, fading from view as the dawn brightened into day.

"Oh," said Sarah with a yawn, "I'm suddenly very sleepy."

"I am, too," said Elizabeth. "But I think that this is going to be the most wonderful Christmas ever."

"So do I," said Sarah as she took her sister's hand. "Better than I ever could have dreamed."